Highest In Command: The Gabrielle Black Chronicles

By-Ann Leona

THIS NOVEL IS A WORK OF FICTION. ANY NAMES, CHARACTERS, PLACES, AND INCIDENTS ARE THE PRODUCT OF THE AUTHOR'S IMAGINATION OR ARE USED FICTITIOUSLY. ANY RESEMBLENCE TO ACTUAL PERSONS LIVING OR DEAD, BUSINESS ESTABLISHMENTS, EVENTS, OR LOCALES IS ENTIRELY COINCIDENTAL. THE PUBLISHER NO THE AUTHOR HAS ANY CONTROL OVER AND DOES NOT ASSUME RESPONSIBILITY FOR THE AUTHOR OR THIRD PARTY WEBSITES OR THEIR CONTENT.

Copyright 2014 Ann Leona Publishing

All rights reserved

ISBN:1499617526

INSBN-13: 978-1499617528

Dedication

This dedication goes to a few people. First is my Grandmother whom lost her battle with Cancer and passed on October 7, 2014. She was my inspiration for my pen name Ann Leona as well as my publishing business that I'm starting. Second is my children Camron and Zackery, they love brag about their Mom and are my biggest supporters always. Third is my sister Kristina, no matter what she makes it her business to read all of the novels that I publish and I love her for that. Lastly, any fans that I may have far and few in between I appreciate you supporting my cause and my rise to a great author one novel at a time! Thanks to you all!

Chapter 1

'Sylas'

Even the best assassins slip up every now and again. We're allowed to have bad days. It's an unwise sacrifice to do so, but even the deadliest of us have been faced with situations that aren't desirable. Looked death in the eyes, grappled with an inevitable possibility of failure. As the leader of a high ranked criminal organization, I am currently faced with such a conundrum. Though every move that is made on my part is planned meticulously and carried out cautiously, it remains to be a fact that I've fucked up. No one knows of this personal revelation and I don't plan on having that change. Upon my journey to arrive at a destination of great power; power that I was born to wield, I managed to fuck up. What better fuck up is there to have than one that involves a woman, huh? My past and my present have to merge momentarily in an effort to create my ideal future. Once that's completed, my past can kiss my ass for all I care. However, nothing in my life is ever so simple. There was hard work involved in expelling me from the womb and into the world. A life was lost in the process and one left behind to fulfill a purpose.

Minos Sylas Tiernan

My mother wanted her first and only son to bear a name that held dominance. A strong male name that exhibits authority and power. So, she graced me with the title of Minos Sylas; its meaning translates to King of the Forest and Woods. Coupled with the name of my family, Tiernan, meaning Lord and Master; my name set me apart from all other men. From the moment of my birth I've had very high standards to live up to. I chose to meet those standards head on in the way that I saw fit. I'd decided early on in life that if I am to be a King, then I'd rather be the King appointed to rule the underworld. The only man strong enough to press upon the lowest of the low and enforce order amidst chaos; I'm good at what I do. I am even greater at the tasks that others aren't even aware that I'm capable of. I'm a well known man, whom no one knows at all. Not even the one woman I've ever felt love for knows me, or as close to love as a man like me can get. I couldn't tell her who I really am all of these years. Not because any of that "for her own good" bullshit either. She couldn't know because I didn't want her to; it's as plain and simple as that. No one can be allowed to read the entire book of Minos Tiernan cover to cover. Letting others in can prove to produce weaknesses within my tightly woven structure. My woman, my Gabrielle; she's no weakness by far. She radiates strength and exudes the same power as I do. It's just never been the time for her to learn more; there's a moment for every revelation to be brought forth and hers hadn't come yet. She's more than proven her worth to me ten times over as of today. Looking at my woman through a one way glass with a frown upon her face and so much animosity in her voice; it distracted me greatly. Her lack of happiness drove a deep urge inside of me to kill someone. It pissed me off to have to push her away as I had, but it's all apart of my plans. Even in the depressive state that I was seeing her in at this moment, she was still far beyond beautiful to me. I'd seen that beauty as soon as I'd laid my eyes on her way back some time ago, even if she couldn't see it herself. It was the African Goddess that I saw when I looked at Gabrielle for the first time. Or maybe she is her reincarnation? When she lay beneath my body, I could feel her pulling forth my soul to devour for her pleasure. Only a short time before that, I'd spotted her inside of a library in a shaded corner on the floor. Her knees were drawn up to her chest and her arms folded around them with a book held tightly within her grasp. A vast array of bound pages were surrounding her on the floor aside her round ass and tiny feet. Full of shy and innocent intelligence; yet underneath the warmth of my body all that I could see was an African Goddess. With each stroke that I delivered to her, my body called to her by many names. Yalode, my woman of wealth. Laketi, my woman who responds so attentively to my touch. Yemaya, my woman whose sensual curves twist and turn like flowing waters. But my mind and my heart know her only as Oshun. Beautiful golden brown eyes; my Oshun. The giver of all love; my woman to bring the order needed to my life. A fucked up life that I've lived greatly as an African King with a curse for the cravings of power and blood. The moment the waters of Gabrielle Black washed over my body I knew she'd be the one by my side when I sat upon my throne above the low lives of the underworld. Not serving as my Queen, but even higher as my Goddess; blessing my path toward greatness. I knew it from the manner in which she rolled her body atop of mines. She was the one... She'd be my secret weapon. She was my Oshun.

Gabrielle

"Oshun"

I slipped up recently. I was hired to assassinate my boss and I let myself love him in the process. I completed the job, killed him with my bare hands and for the first time since I've been in this business I have regrets. The man that I've followed and loved for so long is now a complete stranger to me. He'd included me in his rise in rank to the Highest In Command, but I fear his ulterior motives for doing so. There are many secrets that he's kept from me, including his true identity. Something I still have yet to fully be informed of, but that will change soon enough. While I underestimated Minos' capacity for deception greatly, he also underestimated my aptitude for malevolence. At the exact moment that I crawled into the back seat of my Hummer several weeks ago, I was broken inside. Dejected, confused, battered, bruised, and in pain internally as well as externally; I'd never been so happy to see my half brother in my entire life. Without his care, I'm sure that the insanity that was crowding my brain would've won the fight. The reasonable and rational parts of me were trapped in another dimension so to speak. I had almost completely checked out of "Normalville" in exchange for a ticket to LaLa Land. Minos had summoned me several times to report at what's now my previous check-in location to train for my new position as his second in command. What he didn't know however, was that I no longer inhabited the same safe haven. My brother had cleared the spot and placed a decoy there temporarily in the event that someone was sent to search for me. He'd cleared all avenues to ensure that I wouldn't be found before I wanted to be. Once I'd gathered the strength to make the trip to my previous haven's state to report, Minos was there waiting for me. I could tell that he was taken aback by my appearance. I'd never been one to be neglectful of my looks. Even when I dressed for comfort or convenience, I always did so in an above presentable manner. Entering the private office where our meeting was to be held, I'm sure I resembled a zombie strained and starving during an apocalypse. For one slight moment, after seeing what I wreck I was, I thought I saw the old Sylas that I thought I knew. In a span of about sixty seconds or so, he looked toward me with a deep set of worries displayed on his face. His body language stiffened and I could tell he struggled to straighten himself and return to a manner of indifference. I didn't speak and didn't show any emotion. When he opened his mouth to begin speaking, Minos had replaced Sylas again saying, "It's very apparent that your mental state has been compromised Black. Your assigned date to report has long expired and you're in violation of so many codes that I honestly don't have the time to go over them all given my busy schedule. Given that you're obviously not of sound mind, I'll postpone this meeting and reassign your new duties to another until such time that I can deem you entirely competent to continue serving The Society." Giving no response or sound of understanding, I simply blinked and continued to stare blankly in his direction. After a long pause, looking to me as if he thought I'd speak up to object or argue with him, he continued, "You're to be here tomorrow at 0600 sharp and report to Dr. Shanahann for evaluation. You'll receive further instruction from me on an as needed basis. This meeting is over…" Getting up from his seat, he abruptly left the room without any other words.

I cannot always placate my thoughts and it proves to be difficult to referee the tug of war between my mind and my heart. My life has floated away aimlessly into oblivion. I do not see, I do not hear, my thoughts are cloudy; all I can do is feel. Feel the confusion, the hurt, the anger. Disappointment... I feel the self loathing; an inner struggle with myself over the placement of shame. I have no one else to blame but myself. An acceptance of reality and demotion of any denial should undoubtedly insinuate a step closer to my personal recovery. That couldn't be farther from the truth, however. The completion of my last assignment has served to rid me of the last tidbit of my soul that was remaining. When there is no soul left inside of the living, there is no hope. No light at the end of the tunnel, no optimism, no positivity; only darkness. My blood love was now pumping a vigorous shade of black and my heart craved blood to replace what it'd lost. Instead of pulling me from this deep dark place that I now reside in to put forth the necessary motions needed for my next blood bath; I'd delved deeper into the pit carved for evil. In the wake of my revenge, there will be nothing left aside the many dead bodies and I intend to save the most desired for last.

Broderick

I've never cared for that piece of shit that my sisters taken a liking to. Since the days of our childhood, I've always felt the need the need to protect her. She and I were raised in separate households by different mothers, but fathered by the same man. My mother gave birth to me out of wedlock only a few years after my father's wife had Gabby. A product of a long term affair between my mother and our father, I was the token illegitimate child within his marriage. Mrs. Black was well aware of my mother's existence and she knew of my impending birth just after my mother made the announcement to my father. Yet, she remained by his side and allowed me to be apart of my sister's life throughout our childhood.

She's always been my best friend, I tell her shit that I wouldn't dare utter to anyone else. Gabrielle is the only person that I've fully trusted and she trusts me just as much in return. Admittedly, I was pissed when she told me of her plans to attend a college away from our home state. Those years she was away were hard because I'd been so accustomed to confiding in my older sister for any and everything that happened in my life. Once while I was visiting her in at her apartment in Georgia, she told me that she'd met a man that was akin to being a God in her eyes. Every thought she had of this asshole was shared with me, followed by me sharing my concern and dislike for the way she seemed to worship his existence. Right from the start, I knew Sylas would mean trouble for my sister. Immediately after he'd recruited her into The Society she'd told me and made me swear to secrecy. He'd pulled her into his dangerous world and she'd brought me aboard to be her second eye. No one knew I existed within her family, including Sylas. Growing up, it was made known early on that our father's position in the upper class society was too important for anyone to know of his secret love child. While I was very well taken care of financially by him, play dates with my sister were never public knowledge. We held onto a "don't ask, don't tell" and "keep it within the confines of the family" kind of position. So, I've become accustomed to being behind the scenes. It didn't bother me to help Gabby without being acknowledged. I often worry for her and her choice to live the life that she allowed this man to bestow upon her. When she fell over into the Hummer and I saw the fragile state she was in; I immediately held Sylas responsible and I've wanted him dead since. Now, Gabrielle wanted him dead as well and I'm going to make damn sure we both get what we want.

During Gabby's time away, I'd done a lot of research and uncovered a lot of shit that would prove to aid us in eliminating Sylas once and for all. The one thing that I'm above average at accomplishing is uncovering things that no one wants found. Things that no one else is ever able to discover; as in the deepest secrets. That's my specialty.

• •

An informant that I'd gathered reliable information from on Sylas alerted me to some interesting details on the Highest In Command's personal secretary and assistant. There was a lot more to the wolf in sheep's clothing than meets the eye; just as Gabby had inferred previously. I was asked to meet in a public location to receive more information on Magdeline Burrows and the link between her and Sylas. It had been agreed upon to meet the informant underground in the subway in New York City one week after receiving the message. Once I touched down in New York and dropped my things by the hotel that I'd reserved, I caught a cab across town. After paying the driver with a hefty tip to keep his mouth shut about ever seeing me I made my way down to the train station where the subway was busy with daily commuters. Posting up on a wall out of direct view and attention of others, I waited for my informant to show. It only took ten minutes to spot a lithe figure appearing from the shadows in a corner of the station. She had a large pit bull on a chain leading in front of her and a neutral expression plastered to her beautiful face. This was my first personal encounter with my informant and I was taken aback by how striking she was. I've never seen such an exotic beauty in my life; this woman was stunning at first glance and as equally dangerous in appearance. Her eyes were as light of a golden brown as her skin tone, her hair a natural afro atop her head restrained in a pony tail that gave the look of a crown adorning her skull; her lips were full and inviting to the male eye and the curves of her body wound tightly emulating the figure eight. Everything about her screamed ferocity and warned of danger, yet I couldn't fathom looking away from her for even a split second. When she approached me and spoke, her voice rang a melody that sang of power and elegance simultaneously. *"Bonjur, je suis Zindzhi.* You are Brody I assume?" A simple nod was all I gave so she continued, leading the tone of our meeting, "I have the information you requested *mais je me demande* once you have it in your possession… Will you use it in the proper manner? Monsieur Brody?" I like her style because she almost conjured a smile from my lips to spread across my face.

Almost…"It depends on what your interpretation of the proper manner is Ms. Zindzhi," I say. Then I follow with, "however, you'll have to accept my direct way when I speak bluntly and say that how I use this information is irrelevant and none of your concern ma'am. With all do respect of course." I choose now to smirk, not smile at her; awaiting and anticipating a witty reply, I underestimate this rare beauty greatly in doing so. Zindzhi bouncing straight to the point when she counters, "on the contrary Monsieur Brody it is far from irrelevant. Furthermore, I would also like to inquire what your quarrel is with the man that is linked to the subject listed in this paperwork. Have you been inquisitive merely due to the connection he has with this subject or is there a quarrel as I've assumed?" Damn, her desire to question and debate with me makes her all the more sexy standing her ground while gripping the leash of her hell hound.

"Also, irrelevant and none of your concern…" I offer as my only answer to her interrogation. "How very sad for you Monsieur Brody," she says while she shakes her head and tisks. I offer no response to this, no expression what so ever. Assuming English is my only language, she speaks with her thick accent and says, "*Vous etes en train de creuser des informations qui mettra fin a la vie* Monsieur Brody. *Profitez des dix dernieres minutes de votre vie. Adieu bel home*…Silaha *tuer*!" She says with a slight smile gracing her juicy lips. It only takes a second to translate her words, '*You are digging up information that will end your life Mr. Brody. Enjoy the last ten minutes of your life. Goodbye handsome man… Silaha kill!*' My ego immediately notices that she has called me handsome before it can even register the growling of the bitch hell hound that is now pulling at the chain in her grip in attempt to follow her master's command. Just as she releases her vicious bitch Silaha I manage to unsheathe the machete that I'd concealed underneath my coat. As I readied my stance for the hell hound's attack I see a giant brute of a man step from his hiding place in a shadowed corner. "Shango, *assurez-vous qu'il ne vit pas et nettoyer votre mess*," she says to the man beast as she swiftly walks away and back into the shadows of the subway. Silaha leapt for my throat just as my brain translated her message to ensure my death and I caught the bitch mid air with my blade and continued the force of my blade entrance into the dogs belly to flip the hound over my head and out of my way. Before I had a moment to blink or search for the path that Zindzhi had taken to leave the train station the giant Shango was on my ass. Machete in hand, I awaited his attack. His first move was toward my hand in an attempt to relieve me of my weapon. *Big mistake not so jolly giant*, I thought. As he struggled with my right hand, I used my left to grab the machete sheathed at my back and came around with it intended to cut this son of a bitches head off. Slicing at his neck with my left hand, I noticed that what should have been a gash large enough to half way topple his head ended in only being a small cut. *What the fuck?* I spun and rounded with the weapon I held in my right hand and sliced him a second time. Only a thin stream of blood slid down his neck from the cut. Sharpening my blades regularly was a ritual for me so this freak of nature should be missing a head right now. Instead he was coming at me still, full speed ahead. Before his large body clashed with mines, I dipped my body low dodging our collision. Rounding on the momentum of my body I dug the machete in my left hand into his back and it snapped into; breaking my heavy duty blade with force. Pissed at this supernatural bastard's inability to kill over and die, I drove my other machete into his face right in between his eyes. My blade drove in but not far; Shango bellowed out a roar. I wasn't going to stick around to see if he was okay, that's for damn sure. Broderick Black was far from being a fool. Using his moment of weakness to my advantage, I turned and hauled ass out of the subway and hailed a cab two blocks away. As the cabbie drove away I couldn't help but think, *what the fuck just happened?* I had no idea why my informant spoke the things she did in her native tongue or why she had me attacked after she'd provided me with so much information. But, I sure as hell was going to find out and soon.

■■■

Chapter 2

'Minos'

I met Magdeline Burrows on an assignment that I'd been completing in the Dominican Republic. Born to a Spanish speaking mother with an American father, she was an exotic beauty with a sly smile, a timid physical appearance, and an inner lust for deception. She had sought me out soon after seeing me at the Merengue Festival. I was there tracking an informant that could lead me to sensitive information regarding my target. Not only did she give me her body soon after making her acquaintance, but she also surrendered control of her mind and life. I took her as my lover and moved her to the states for one definite purpose. Not long after our initial encounter, I discovered she possessed serious manipulative behaviors. Full of lies and deceit; she was fueled by the demise of others. The only way to explain her disposition is that she got her rocks off by observing the terrible fates of those who fell susceptible to her conniving plots and plans. However, falling in love with me was her biggest mistake to date. Even though it was clear to her that I would never love her as she wishes I would; she's remained in my corner for much longer than I'd like to admit. At a time when she was young and eager to please, I arranged to have her gain employment within The Society. The former leader of our organization saw in her the exact same deception that I saw and he immediately took her under his wing to better use her for his own agenda. It was originally her idea to remove Gerard from our ranks and place me at the top of the totem pole. I'd previously thought to wait him out until his retirement to take over his position. Maggie introduced the idea of forcing him into retiring instead. She believed it would gain my love and seal her position beside me rather than behind me. By then however, I'd met Gabrielle, my good luck charm. Just as Oya kept her lover from Oshun in the old African tale, Maggie intended to counter the connection that I shared with Gabby. She was full of resentment for the one woman who was able to place a warm spot inside of my cold heart; a feat that she herself hadn't accomplished. Once I placed a firm grip of control upon Magdeline she pretended to submit to following the plans I'd put in place. But, I knew she was full of shit. As soon as the opportunity presented itself, my modern day Oya would attempt to lock me away for her own selfish needs and seek to destroy what she saw as competition. This fact is what's caused her ultimate demise to become a sealed fate. The decision had already been made on my part to eliminate Maggie from the equation once she's completely served her purpose. It isn't beyond my notice that she's been a great help towards accomplishing my rise in the ranks. But, she hasn't proved to be important enough for me to give a shit about her being alive or dead. Merely a pawn to a majorly cold hearted son of a bitch; she's responsible for failing to notice that her end was near. It's not my job to feel remorse for her stupidity. Never completely trust a spy or assassin; because our way to the top is mostly always a carved path covered in others blood.

Magdeline

'Oya'

The moment I saw Gabrielle enter The Veil, dangled as bait in front of Gerard's line of view, I knew I wanted to be the one to kill her. Seeing her appearance at The Society's headquarters right on schedule as planned; I'd initially thought that she was no threat against my agenda. She seemed so mundane, so ordinary, with her dark skin and petite frame. Nothing but the light brown color of her eyes made her stand out. I've never understood what Minos could see so special in her that he didn't see in me. All too glad to allow her to replace my duties of sucking Gerard's dick on the regular, I made sure to remain in the shadows within The Veil. Those were my designated play times after all and I wasn't about to allow that bitch to spoil my fun in any way shape or form. Honestly speaking, I didn't think she'd be able to pull off the hit and I told Minos so. He'd constantly bragged at how "skilled" she was with her assignments, but doubt crowded my brain from the start. I could've easily held her position and done the job better than she, but Minos insisted that I wasn't meant for the field. As soon as Bontaeu allotted me the position as his personal assistant I began to manipulate his trust. There was no doubt in my mind then that Minos deserved to serve as the leader he was destined to be; I stand by that declaration on this day. We were meant to run shit, he as a firm leader and I at his side as a confidant. No way in hell am I allowing that bitch Gabby to rob me of my place and power. When Minos told me that he didn't love me that shit hurt me momentarily and it discouraged me just a bit as well. I told myself that as time went along he'd grow to love me and when shit gets real I've got a bullet with Gabrielle's name tattooed all over it. Right now Minos and I are merely partners; I play the role that he's asked me to so that he feels like he's in control. Soon enough though, we'll be so much more. The Veil was placed under my control and demand after Gerard Bontaeu was retired. Serving as an unseen but strongly respected and heard owner, I used the private club to function as more than a place to unwind and play. Packages of cocaine by the brick were being brought over by some of my cousins from The Dominic. Once it passed over the waters and was delivered to a discreet location, a large portion was sold and distributed to the patrons of The Veil. My intentions were to keep them so high that spending all of their "rich old geezer" money wouldn't even process as anything near a thought in their minds. The remainder of the cocaine shipment was stretched, divided, delivered to hand-to-hand street hustlers, and sold to the less than fortunate bastards in every hood in the surrounding areas of Louisiana. With the bundles of money the club made on membership dues alone, I found an opportune loop hole in which to launder thousands upon thousands of dollars through the private bank accounts of my new establishment. Ensuring that once my plans fell into place Minos and I would never run low on financial gain. We were already financially stable, but a woman had to be sure to stash away her own nest egg. Never allow a man to be your only meal ticket; especially one with the mind frame that Sylas had. He was all about business first, and anything or anyone else came second or didn't come at all. That's one of the most important things that my *Abuela* taught me as a child and I intended to take heed to that lesson fully.

The first thing I needed to do was pull that leech Gabby away from Minos and permanently remove her from the picture. I'm feeling cramped with her inside of my plans and frankly I'm just tired of seeing the bitches face. So, I put the plans in motion to remove such a nuisance from my path and this Earth. My brother Armand wasn't a hit man by far, but he was damn good at making unwanted things and people disappear. Anything that stood in my path quickly disappeared once my eldest brother caught wind of it. I never asked him any questions and I always ensured that he got a nice gift delivered to him each time one of my problems vanished. We had a detailed discussion about Minos' little pet assassin and when I left my family's home I felt better knowing that soon I'd be one step closer to my rightful seat next to The Highest In Command. Once Gabrielle is out of the way I'm sure I can have Minos eating out of the palm of my hand while wound tightly around my middle finger in no time.

AidaTiernan

'Zindzhi'

My father always told my brother and me never to fall in love unless it was absolutely necessary. Our family is one that descends from a long existence of powerful people. We are distant spawns of Kings and Queens, heroes and villains, royal and humble souls alike. No generation of our family has lived a life of poverty; we have always existed within the lines of wealth and privilege. Given the surname Tiernan, you are destined for greatness in one manner or another. As my mother's first born, I was allotted a name that spoke of my destiny to protect any siblings that came after me upon any demise that my parents could befall. Aida, pronounced *ah-ee-dah*, translates to mean "*princess*". Zindzhi translates to mean "*warrior*". Princess Warrior Lord and Master; I am told that my title is befitting of my life. I have walked this Earth for thirty-seven years and have yet to fall in love with any man. No man is upon an identical level of intelligence as I. Save the men of my family; no man can equal my devious demeanor. My brother Minos isn't as keen to follow the parental advice given to us. He has fallen in love with a woman whose nature is similar to his own. She hinders his growth, but he sees her as an extension to allow him to reach his ultimate success swiftly. This woman will bring the end to him prematurely and I've told him so numerous times over. I'm to be careful of how I speak to Minos because his interest in this woman, this Gabrielle, it brings about conflict within him. There wasn't too much thought involved in my revelation that I must steer the reigns of my brother's life gently so as to not alert him to my presence. He won't listen to me directly, so I must ensure that he doesn't allow a female to wreak havoc onto his rise to greatness. There has been a man inquiring about this Gabrielle that Minos has become so smitten with. Merely a case of pup love, but he pursues it still. This man is Brody, upon my intercepting his inquiries he briefly gave mention of my brothers name. He says my brothers play toy Magdeline is poison to this Earth; this is a fact that I've previously deduced. Had she been more than a sexual object to Minos I'd have pried further into eliminating her. However, my brother has assured me she is merely but a means of entertainment for a man as he sows his seeds of power. Once his has tired of the meager play toy, he will dispose of her accordingly. A bitter taste has entered my mouth upon the revelation that this man Brody is questioning members of many organizations for information on Minos Tiernan. My duty is to protect the only sibling that my parents birthed. I am in tune to every criminal organization that operates world wide; this may seem to be an impossibility to an average pawn in the game of chess. Impossible isn't apart of my vocabulary at present. My position at current is running the largest drug trade in operation. Distributing large quantities of cocaine, marijuana, and various forms of pills on all seven continents via several minions that drag below the feet of the Princess Warrior Lord and Master. One of my biggest buyers in the Dominican Republic alerted my second in command of a price upon Gabrielle's head. Shortly thereafter, disguising myself as an informant for financial gain, I fed this information to Brody and setup a time that we would meet for an exchange. He thought he was to come deliver my payment and I would deliver information to him on Magdeline. The plan was to eliminate Brody, thus erasing any obstacles that would impede my brother's path. I made the journey to America and brought one of my best men, Shango, along. Shango always made a mess of his victims, but that's what I desired. I wanted to send a message to whomever Brody was working for or with that Minos Tiernan was off limits in the crime circles. They would know that he has unknown allies in the highest factions of the criminal world. Initially I'd imagined this Brody character to be of low status; he was ringing the bells of all of the wrong doors, so he couldn't be too wise. What I hadn't bargained for however, was to arrive in New York and in the shadows of the subway capture my first glimpse at a man so handsome that he made my heart strum a lively tune. The tiny muscle encased within my chest had never pulled so tightly on my being. It was an enormous shame that his death had been predetermined to arrive on that day. When I stepped from the shadows and experienced the audio of his voice, I felt a flush of heat and moisture in the nether regions of my body. My muscles clenched and my breath caught in my throat momentarily. There was something about this man, this Brody with the magical voice that brought life to my heart that had never had a chance to breathe until now. He was familiar, yet a single stranger capturing my attention in the deadliest of ways. Unfortunately, I held firm that he must die then and there. Silaha, one of my pet beasts had been along to serve as a distraction. Upon giving the order to my beast Silaha, I imprinted a vision of Brody into my mind and turned away. As I stalked back into the shadows, I gave Shango his orders and melded into the shadows never looking back. Before I made my leave from America, I arranged a private meeting with my brother. I had no intentions of telling him every revelation that had surfaced, but I informed him that the object of his affection had numbered days ahead of her. Minos did not comment on this information any beyond a nod to me. Kissing my forehead he whispered, "*Merci, Aida. Je t'aime.*" I gave a slight nod to my kin saying, "*De rien, je t'aime aussi Minos.*" There was still much loose rope that needed severing, after giving my brother my love I traveled to the airport for my flight. Clearing any obstructions from our pathways were my primary intentions, but some obstructions just didn't die when they were supposed to.

Chapter 3

'Sylas'

I received a call from my older sister Aida that she was in the states and it was urgent that we meet at a secure location. She met me at one of my safe havens in Colorado; Aida was the only person I trusted with the location of any of my safe havens and even she didn't possess knowledge of all of them. Yes, I have many places to escape to when I want or need to disappear. There are no men like me, but if there were they'd require several avenues of escape to keep enemies guessing. When Aida reached my cabin, she greeted me upon entry with a look of the stern persuasion. This was no tale of her mood or an intention for our meeting for stern was her general disposition. "*Bonjour* Minos," she said as she kissed my cheek. "Greetings Aida, to what do I owe the pleasure of your presence here in America?" I asked my sister sincerely. "I have news for you brother," she says. "It seems that I was correct in deducing that your pup love would prove to be a toxic one for you and your Gabrielle." This caught my attention right away and my ears perked as I listened intently to hear what she'd say next. Raising my eyebrow so she'd continue I waited on her news to spill. "There has been a price placed upon your Gabrielle's life Minos. A man hailing in the Dominican Republic has leaked information within my drug channels of a hit he is to complete. The man is called Armand and he is a mouthy one of low descent. He is a minion of channels in The Dominic, Columbia, and Brazil." She paused in speaking to absorb my reaction to this news. I offered her none; it is unbecoming of a man of power to exhibit emotion. Knowing me all too well, her expression spread with a slight smirk of her lips. Inside I was filled with rage and anger. Who the fuck would draw enough audacity to price one of my assassins? A price upon the head of my Gabby, my Oshun... In a neutral tone I asked my sister, "Who contracted the price?" Just then Aida smiled something no one observes of her often. "Oh, you're going to enjoy this brother," she stated wickedly. "The price is not formally contracted by a faction or even an organization for that matter. It was directly ordered by the sibling below Armand and their family name is Burrows." That shit managed to make my jaw twitch and my rage tick at an unimaginable pace. Aida lost her smile and spoke on to say, "Your little play toy Magdeline has ordered the price Minos. I don't think she appreciates having competition too well. You see, this is the poison I spoke of with you some time ago brother." She shook her head slowly in front of me as I clenched my jaw so tightly that I thought my teeth would shatter at any moment. "Never fall in love, that is what was ingrained into your mind Minos and you disobeyed valuable parental advice. For centuries love has proven to be a grand distraction to our ancestors Minos. Yet, you felt the need to learn this lesson in a difficult manner that will ultimately end with feeling the hard stinging pain that love brings forth." Inhaling deeply and then calmly exhaling I gathered my composure. There was no way in hell I would stand for such an insult as Magdeline had placed upon me. Her brother would be dealt with and then I'd ensure that Magdeline would be buried alive for such treachery. I was full aware that she thought herself in charge of our situation, but I'd underestimated her stupidity greatly. Just as well, she had underestimated my unyielding wrath when challenged. Speaking a word of gratitude and love to my only sister I kissed her head saying, "*Merci, Aida. Je t'aime.*" Aida returned the sentiment and left my safe haven with the air of confidence that she always carried with her head poised high. My fuck ups were becoming more evident unfortunately for me; my sister had intercepted the plot of my biggest mistake to date. That mistake was named Magdeline Burrows and once her schemes were dealt with, she would also be in the most torturous way possible.

Aboard the jet after I'd left my safe haven I made several calls to locate this minion Armand. It didn't take me long to gather intelligence on him; Aida was correct in saying he was mouthy. This lowlife liked to gossip more than a teen in high school. That always led to an end to any criminal's lifespan. A connect of my sisters gave information leading me to a drop that Armand was expected to receive in Brazil two days from now. I'd thought to send one of my elite to rid me of this infestation, but I personally wanted to issue his termination. The face of Minos Tiernan would be the last that he'd see before he plunged into the darkness of hell. Two days didn't give me much advance time to push my schedule around but anything could be rearranged accordingly. Pulling my cell out I called Magdeline and calmly told her to reschedule my calendar for the week. "Is there an engagement that I failed to notate Minos?" Magdeline asked of me. "No," I said. "Someone of great importance has called in a favor I owe to be delivered in France. This will be off record, please note my time to be scheduled for R and R. No other information is needed and I am not to be disturbed during my time away. Also, ensure that my calendar reflects such." Then, I simply ended the call.

A couple of days later I was back in the jet headed to South America. Brazil to be exact; I intended to intercept the hit placed on Gabby before anyone found her and made good on Magdeline's plans. It didn't require much effort to find Armand, he and his low budget thugs were all over the place from the moment I struck out on my mission. The streets were teaming with coked up have-nots lingering for their spot in line to re-up on the impeding product dropping. No one offered a façade in this bunch; it was obvious even for the untrained eye that illegal activity was afoot and it proved important to those bold enough to wait. Making sure to blend in, yet appear as discreet as a fly on the wall; I kept my ears and eyes open for an opportune seed to sow. One particular man of Spanish descent, appearing to be Puerto Rican, stood with a group of his comrades. He wasn't very tall, 5'6 at the most but he was built with a frame that I assume was freshly received in a local penitentiary. I'm sure this guy won't live long given his propensity of running his mouth to any other who offered attentions to his efforts to prove his manliness. Someone would shoot him in his mouth to shut him up and I gathered his end would be soon if not before he made leave from Brazil. Speaking partly in English and part Spanish I heard him gloat. "Yo, mi padre is tight with this connect here. He put me on, after this drop; my come up will have these punta's deep on my dick yo!" He bellowed out a laugh before continuing, "Word is my man organizing this drop likes to blow his cabesa with that good shit. If you want to get on let me know, mi padre arranged for us to meet at his hotel and test his shit out." Young fucking amateurs; I'd kill him myself for being so stupid but he was one of many insignificant shells roaming the planet. Standing there for only a moment longer listening to a few more people, I casually walked away formulating additions to my original plans.

●●●

One hour later Armand was conducting the necessary business for his drop and I was inside of his hotel waiting for him to return. I rarely composed hits that required me to be this close to a mark anymore. A bullet in the head or some other discreet method of demise was my usual repertoire, but this was personal. When Armand entered his mediocre hotel suite I was positioned in a crevice behind the door that was meant to serve as a closet. Standing as still as a statue, I counted down as the hotel door slowly crept to a close. Waiting; wanting him to see his end coming. Armand removed his hat and turned to place it in the tiny closet and as soon as he turned toward the direction of danger I made my move. Before he was allotted a moment to register any form of shock or surprise regarding the danger that he was facing I'd began my attack. Palm flat, fingers extended, I struck him in his throat in one swift move. Then followed with a blow to his throat with my fist, damaging his trachea offering him difficulty to scream or breathe. He grabbed at his neck and stumbled backwards three steps. Sweeping his legs from under him, I forced him to the ground quickly and swiftly. Grabbing the needle from my suit pocket that I'd placed there earlier, I popped the cap off and pressed my knee firmly in his chest so he couldn't move. "Don't worry, Armand. You won't be in hell alone for long; Magdeline will be joining you very soon." His eyes grew wide and I plunged the needle containing enough pure and uncut heroin to kill someone three times his size into his neck. Squeezing to release the poison, I smiled internally and externally at his plight. It didn't take long for his body to begin to seize and foam escaped from his mouth. Dragging him by his shirt collar as his body went through its process of shutting down from being overwhelmed with the drug; I pulled him to the bedside. As I flipped him over to position his body, I heard the tale sign of death's cry. The death rattle rose from his throat and curdled deeply as his bowels released and the devil pulled him into the depths of darkness. "*Je vous verrai en enfer Armand. Je serai celui assis sur le trone.*"

Gabrielle

Got an urgent message from Broderick just as the imbecile Dr. Walter Shanahann was signing off on my release from his services for Minos. In short the message he was telling me to get the fuck from The Society's underground fortress. There'd been a hit placed on my life and he's received concrete assurance that the hit was ordered by none other than Magdeline Burrows. "THEY'RE GOING TO RETIRE YOU GABBY. GET THE FUCK OUT OF THERE NOW! MEET ME AT EMERGENCY C IMMEDIATELY," was the remainder of the message. Distrust was never a word I associated with my brother's name and I didn't disbelieve his warning or the urgency in which I should take heed. However, I did not flinch at this revelation in the least bit. I'd thought I was being set up all along. Somehow, I knew the assignment that I was given on Gerard Bontaeu was the beginning of a meaning to my end. Dr. Shanahann had turned his back to deliver his official seal to the release form which had given me the moment to read Brody's message. When he turned back to my direction, my phone had already been stowed away and my mind was already reeling to plan a timely exit. "It has been quite the displeasure speaking with you the whole while Agent Black. I will be sporadically monitoring your ongoing progress as you return to the field," the stubby lump of man meat said to me. I didn't smile nor nod, nor offer him a response as was the behavior he was accustomed to me exhibiting. After a moment of silence he uttered, "Well then… Good day." Grabbing the official document of my freedom from his asinine assessments of me, I strolled from his office. A meeting had been scheduled with The Highest In Command for the following day to follow up with my orders granted I obtained the necessary release from Shanahann. Once I had finally reached the threshold on the upper levels of the compound, I had no intentions on returning to The Society. Every inch of my fiber and intuition knew that Brody's warning to me was warranted. So, once I arrived onto the private landing area at the airport; I entered the back seat of my black sedan and had the driver take me to a drop off point. When I arrived at the crowded public area I hailed a cab across town to a second discreet location. After arriving, I walked several blocks to a not so nearby parking garage and went directly to the location of a Chevy Camaro that was parked on the third level. Black paint, black interior, deep colored tinting on the windows; this was my transportation to meet my brother. Reaching underneath the car, I ran my hand along the bottom and found the key hidden in a tiny case.

Three minutes later I was exiting the lot behind a Porsche and within five minutes my Chevy was gliding on the highway toward safety.

Brody and I had set up several means for escape in case of an emergency; along with mapping out several routes in which to travel and even more secret locations that only he and I were privy to. "Emergency C" was a plan we'd orchestrated for when the proverbial shit had hit the fan. There were only two levels of emergency below C, so I knew whatever Brody had discovered was of dire importance. Hours later, I arrived first to my newly located safe haven. I couldn't very well travel to a secret location while Sylas was tracking my every move via the chip located under my skin. There was always shit hindering my process to make it out of this bullshit Sylas has buried atop me and remain with my life in tact. Once I was deep under the cement walls of my safe haven, I entered and locked my system to high level security. As soon as this occurred my cell charmed with a message from Sylas. "YOU'VE DISAPPEARED FROM THE MAP AGENT. WHERE ARE YOU? PROTOCAL STATES YOU MUST BE AVAILABLE BLACK SO IF YOU AREN'T DEAD YOU DAMN WELL BETTER REAPPEAR IN THE NEXT FIVE MINUTES!" I simply ignored his threats and continued with my task at hand. Brody had left me a package inside. One that he and I had been anticipating after the changes that Minos had ensued upon me post my election to the council. Washing and sterilizing my hands first, I opened the package and lay all of its contents in front of me in the bathroom. Snapping my sterile hospital gloves onto my hands first, I sat spread eagle on the floor in front on my ceiling to floor mirror. For whatever reason, the chip was always easier to locate and prominent in revealing it's place after

I'd orgasmed. So, using my vibrator I rubbed teased and tickled my clit at a steady pace until I reached my peak. Just as I saw the fireworks and felt the rush and pop of my sexual release; I dropped the tiny bullet and immediately perused my groin area for the chip. It was in the crevice of my thigh parallel to my clitoris yet closer to my leg than vagina. Holding my finger firm I located the syringe of lidocaine and administered four tiny bee sting shots of it around the area where the chip was located under my finger. Immediately after the numbing medication took effect I chose a scalpel from the layout and sliced open my skin just above where I'd found the chip. Blood poured from the cut, but I proceeded with my task still. Using my index finger and thumb I gently pushed the skin back that I'd cut and the chip was just there in plain sight. Thanking the creator that the slimy black market doctor hadn't dug it too deep into my crouch, I grabbed a set of tweezers from the pack. Being sure to hold steady with both hands; I pinched one end of the tiny chip and pulled it free. My initial thought was to destroy the damn thing but my intuition told me I may need it in the future for my own personal use. So, I sat the chip aside on the sterile pack of paper. I was feeling quite woozy from the stream of blood pouring from the cut so, I grabbed a suture needle and stitched the cut close with dissolvable thread. When I finished mending the tiny cut I placed a bandage there, took an antibiotic to prevent infection later and chased it with a Percocet and energy drink. Hey, I've done worse in the middle of my plight for survival than this shit. Cleaning up the mess I'd made quickly, I placed the tiny chip in a plastic zip lock bag and left it on my desk in the security room. It wouldn't be pinpointed by Sylas here at my underground haven so it was best to leave it. Inside of my arms room I grabbed a few essentials and a couple of "big girl toys" to load into my hummer. Never leave as you came and always assume you are being watched; because more than likely you are every moment of the day. Though I wanted a method of travel to be one with speed, I also needed a ride that would withstand force if I encountered any. My Hummer was always the perfect means for travel in these situations; it had been upgraded to bulletproof in its entirety with several other beneficial features. Once my ride was loaded and ready I opted for a quick change of attire and made leave from my new safe haven. For the second time since I'd been in the field, I was unsure when I'd be able to return to my haven.

After hours of driving on the highway I arrived at location Emergency C. The outer appearance was of a barn in a large expanse of land with overgrown foliage.

Beneath this barn however, was something entirely different. As he was expecting my arrival, when I pulled near, Brody opened the doors to the large two story barn and I pulled my Hummer inside. Slowly as I drove toward the rear a ramp appeared from beneath my truck allowing me access to drive underground to park. If my brother was good at nothing else, he was surely skilled at ensuring we weren't found if he so desired. I pulled my Hummer alongside his black Land Rover and hopped out awaiting entry through the metal doors. When doors slid back, my baby brother Brody was there with a look of relief on his face. "For fucks sake, I've not been happier to see you," he said as he grabbed me and pulled me into his large chest for a bear hug. "Yeah, I love you too Broderick. What's going on? Tell me what you know till this point and we'll take it from there little Bro." Releasing me from his crushing embrace, he turned and led me deeper into the compound of Emergency C carrying a deep look of concern. Traveling down the corridor, we passed several rooms until we reached the end where our security room was located. Emergency C was our largest underground location; there was only one level when going down, but the space spread hundreds of square feet across the fields above. "You're going to want to sit down for this one Gabby," he warned me and I sat in a chair next to him at a medium conference table placed in the center of the security room. Broderick leaned back in his chair and began, "First of all, I'm glad I warned you in a timely manner and that you're okay." Offering my brother a sincere smile of my eyes I said, "I am okay, thank you for making sure of that." He continued, "Straight to the facts... There's a price on your head. I'd been perusing the channels for information on what we'd discussed after your promotion to second in command. After following leads with several different people, I thought I'd come upon concrete information on Magdeline and possibly more information on who Sylas really is and his background in Africa." Raising my eyebrows, I replied, "Thought?" He held his hand up to stop my questioning and kept speaking, "Yes, thought and it turns out that the information on Magdeline is accurate and useful." He paused then said, "Where I ran into resistance is when what I thought was an informant offered to deliver intelligence on Magdeline and offer what she knew of Sylas before he came to America." Wait, did he just say she? My brother knew I was growing anxious so he kept hashing the details to me, "I went to New York to meet this informant, she asked for a large sum of cash in exchange for what she knew about Sylas. We'd agreed to meet in the subway and once she'd handed me the paperwork on Maggie, she issued me a warning. Her features were exotic and she spoke mostly in French with a deep accent when she used English. She was obviously of African descent; she warned me that inquiring intelligence about Sylas was going to get me killed and then she proceeded to carry out that threat." Surprise registered onto my face, "What?" I blurted and narrowed my eyes. Again, she held his hands up to silence me, "Let me tell you this in its entirety, you need to listen intently." Sitting back, I nodded for him to continue. "There was a mutant mutt she had on a chain with her that I killed; I didn't know initially that she also had what appeared to be a mutant man hiding in the shadows with her as well. He was a giant fucking African and when I drove my blade into his skin during his attack, it barely affected him. So, I bailed the fuck out and quickly. This woman introduced herself to me as Zindzhi. I knew immediately that I'd heard that name before, so when I arrived here I did a little research. It turns out that I was right, I'd heard that name within the channels of every major drug ring that I've done business with. Zindzhi is the largest distributor of any product you need worldwide. She is said to be ruthless and cold and I was right when I deduced that she hails from Africa." The wheels that turned the clock inside of my mind started to spin. Brody was going somewhere with this that was impertinent in our plight, but my brain wasn't catching up as fast as I needed it to. "Wait, so what does this have to do with Sylas? As far as I know he doesn't have business within the drug factions," I asked my brother. He sat up and leaned closer to me saying, "Zindzhi is the name that this woman is widely known by within the channels. But, as you know finding out what is what and who is who is what my specialty is big sister. The woman's true name is Aida Tiernan; Zindzhi is her middle name. She's Minos' older sister Gabby." For the first time since I attended the board meeting after my last assignment, I was at a loss for words. Apparently I looked as dumbfounded as I felt because my brother quickly spoke up saying, "That's not where this ends Gabby. The price that was issued for you was ordered by Maggie and I've been told her brother, Armand, is the man who was to execute the hit. But, when I attempted to find Armand so that I could have that motherfucker snuffed out; I found out that someone had already beaten me to the punch." Still trying to work this shit out and wrap my brain around it all, I remained quiet. "Dude was found in Brazil; overdosed on heroin but the shit looks more than it seems to me. There's a lot of shit going on behind the scenes Gabby that apparently you have taken a blind eye in the past and I'm guessing it's due to the trust you had for that asshole. There's got to be a reason as to why Magdeline would place a hit on you and I'm guessing that reason is Minos Tiernan." My brain was retracing the years I'd spent worshipping the ground that Sylas walked on and counting how long he'd probably been planning this unbeknownst to me. I was starting to retreat back into my darkest place; I'd been checked out for weeks following my last hit and I damn well wasn't going back there for sure. Not without a fight this time around. First on my list of thoughts was that bitch Magdeline Burrows or the bitch of the former once I was finished with her. Before completing our talk and his update on all that had been happening while I lay back within the walls of The Society and listened as Dr. Shanahann tried to brainwash me; Broderick gave me the paperwork that Zindzhi had given him on Maggie. Obviously she hadn't planned on him being alive long enough to do anything with the information. People always seemed to fail in "overstanding" my baby brother and I which proved to be their grandest mistake. According to Zindzhi's information, Magdeline Burrows was known within her birthplace as *La Guera Loca*, which translates roughly to "the crazy blonde." Maggie and her eldest brother Armand were con artists and low level drug pushers who fancied themselves as being professional criminals. However, it seems that they were no more than two puppets following behind the wagging tales of the real professionals. It didn't make any sense to me why Sylas would have Maggie order the price for my life when he had so many connections that he could contract my hit and no one would be brave enough to look even once in his direction. None of this was connecting properly to me and I didn't know how and why this bitch was involved with Minos beyond his position as Highest In Command. The one thing that I did know for sure was that the prissy bitch was going to die and I would make sure it's at the hands of the *Black Widow*.

●●

Broderick and I had mapped out a plan that wasn't failsafe but, we would attempt to make it work anyhow. We were hoping that Maggie's death would draw Sylas to where we needed him and then our plan got very complicated from there. Eliminating Minos' little assistant bitch was the easy part; killing Minos himself would prove to be the test of my better abilities. We'd learned that Magdeline had returned to The Dominic for her brother's burial and would return to the states the following week. I'd use that as my opportunity since air travel was too risky due to the eyes that Minos had everywhere. There was a plan that my brother had concocted to lure Magdeline into my web and into the end of her lifespan.

Chapter 4

'Minos'

As I watched Magdeline exit The Society's private jet, my jaw clenched tight at the very presence of her. She slid into the limousine and displayed a look of shock on her face. "Minos, I didn't realize you'd be greeting me on escort to The Society. I've had such a tiempo difícil with my brother's death. I'm glad to see you mi amor," she said. Destining her voice, I simply nodded; she looked at me blankly as if she knew there was something going awry. As the limousine pulled away from the airport, I noticed a car tailing us. I didn't have time for this shit. Keeping my eye on the driver's side mirror, I quickly noticed the car to be Gabrielle's black Hummer. I tried to contact her and was given a message that she'd blocked her smart phone. A few messages to Zinzhi and several clicks and avenues later; I was connected to Gabby's smart phone. With my sisters help I'd bypassed her block and broke her secure connection to outsiders. This message is what I sent to her in quote, "GABBY I SEE YOU BEHIND ME. I WANT THE SAME THING YOU DO, I WANT MAGGIE DEAD. I'LL GIVE YOU THE COURTESY OF MAKING HER DISAPPEAR. I KNOW WHAT SHE DID TO YOU AND IT WASN'T AT MY HANDS OR ORDER. WE WILL END AT HER PLACE AND YOU CAN DO AS YOU PLEASE WITH HER FROM THERE ON. I WILL LEAVE AND NOT RETURN. I DO CARE MORE THAN YOU KNOW- SYLAS"

....

I ordered the driver to route to Maggie's address. "You know what I need always. Acouple days of rest and I'll be fully restored and back at The Society as if I'd never left." I smiled at her so she would not know anything was afoot. She placed a soft kiss upon my lips and I carressed her hair as I gave her a deep and passionate kiss that was my goodbye to her exitense. When Magdeline exited the car and stopped to see that I didn't follow she frowned deeply. "You mean you're not joining me?" she whined "Unfortunately no, I've got important business to attend to that cannot be postponed and the consequences for an absence are dire in nature." I told her. Poking out her bottom lip she frowned once more and exited the vehicle alone walking toward the entrance to her penthouse apartment. I would not miss her. Would not mourn after her death. From this moment henceforth she wasn't even a memory that existed in my world. She was void. Next on my agenda was to find out who this man was who'd been scrounging for information about me.

Zinzhi had said he appeared to be professional; not a minion working for a higher up. My sister had said he'd introduced himself as Brody. I'd never heard of that name in any of the criminal organizations or lower factions. Whereever he hailed from, he'd just made my shit list and that list was one that ended in nothing other than death.

Gabrielle

'La Guera Loca'

I received a text from Sylas, somehow he'd overridden the blocks of security that I'd placed on my smart phone's system. I read the message to Broderick to see what he thought of the warning Sylas heeded and whether it were fiction or truth. "There's only one way to find out big sister and that entails following them and being prepared for war." Sure enough when the limo stopped only Maggie left it; she lingered for a moment and then the limo smoothly drove off. "This could still be a trap Gabby, be cautious," my brother said. When she neared the elevator we waited a bit and then pulled into the parking garage. "I got this," I said to Brody. He gave me an *'are you sure'* look and I nodded while I loaded a few necessaries. Upon entering the elevator I saw it had to lower from the penthouse to retrieve me in the parking garage. Once I was there I didn't sneak to her door, didn't walk softly or briskly; I wanted the bitch to know that I was coming for her and her life. I rang the bell and politely said, "room service, you have a bouquet of flowers from a Mr. Tiernan." Dumb bitch quickly swung open the door in mid sentence, "He's so…" Before sweet had formed onto her lips I'd punched her, busting her mouth and scraping her teeth on my knuckles. Hey, casualties of the job. Maggie stumbled and ran to attack me; I straightened my arm, braced my shoulder and swept her legs from underneath her. Maggie's head hit the hardwood floor beneath her with a thump. Ready for her to give up and me to finish my job I hovered over her saying, "Put a price on my head bitch! And you thought Sylas would let his sweet little pussy lap pet go free? I'm here to euthanize you cunt!" Thinking this was the end she pulled her knees far back into her chest and kicked me with a force so strong that I flew into the wall across from me. "You don't know who I am bitch? In Dominica they call me *La Guera Loca* and I'm one blonde who's crazier than your simple ass will ever have known. You chose the wrong *perra loca* to fuck with today! And I know it was you who killed my *hermano*, I'm going to make you pay for that *puta!*" she carried on and on with her threats to me. I was growing tired of this fucking superhero dialogue so I unsheathed the blade I had at my right side and threw it, landing directly in the middle of her chest. She grasped the knife at her chest as if she could remove it and looked in shock at its presence. Unsheathing the machete that hung at my left side I threw it; landing directly in the center of her forehead. My, oh my had I made a mess of her body. I grabbed the knife wedged into her midsection and pulled it upward while twisting it to shred her insides just for shits and giggles. I grabbed the machete and swung once, then twice; decapitating her head completely from her body. Doing this not to be ruthless, but mainly because I've despised the bitch since the day I first laid my eyes upon her perky smile and her bleach blonde hair. Grabbing my smart phone I called Broderick to let him know that it was clean up time. When he arrived at Magdeline's apartment he shook his head at me and laughed. "Did you have to make such a mess Gabrielle? I think you enjoy making my job even the slightest more difficult." He said to me staring with a *bad girl* face. I simply shrugged my shoulders and said, "What can I say? The cunt had it coming to her; she got what she deserved." We didn't bother to clean up the blood, when her family came looking for her missing body; we wanted them to receive the message that some organizations aren't to be fucked with. Magdeline lived on the top floor in the penthouse making it easy for us to carry her body directly from the elevator into the parking garage. We first destroyed all of the security cameras for the building and elevator lift. Then Brody stood with the body at the lift while I eyed the garage for witnesses and backed the Hummer to the door. We threw her limp body along with her head in the trunk and casually made our way away from Magdeline's past apartment building. From there Broderick drove us to a construction yard. "I've got some connects here that owe me a few favors. They can't afford to snitch, so don't worry a bit." I was looking a bit weary but, I trusted my brother in the upmost. He drove the Hummer around a few large piles of dirt and a few trailers behind the large piles. Beyond the trailers there was another large pile dug deep enough to bury and elephant and there beside it was a large slash machine. Backing the Hummer up to the slash machine, Brody popped the trunk. A few burly men walked up to the back of the vehicle and helped Broderick lift Maggie's body; with the carpet rolled around it and all. They then tossed her dead body rolled into the carpet into the front of the slash machine then her head afterward. The machine grinded and made a large noise for a moment and on the opposite side or end of the machine I saw the bits and pieces of what remained of Magdeline Burrows body filling the deep hole aside of the machine. I didn't frown or say goodbye or even so much as spit on her remains. With a neutral expression upon my face I simply walked back to my Hummer while the men began to fill the hole over that held the remains of my enemy's body.

■■■

My brother and I were taking the Hummer to our underground haven Emergency C where a trusted source would pick the Hummer up from parked inside of the barn and have it reupholstered and cleaned of the blood. I wondered the whole time why Sylas has contacted me and led me to Magdeline to be disposed of. It had to be a trick, I was sure of it and so was Brody. First I destroyed my smart phone since it had been comprised and replaced it with one of many that we kept especially for these situations. Was there a chance that Sylas cared for me in some indirect way? He took it upon himself to hand Maggie over to me, but why? I spoke briefly with Broderick and of course he dismissed the thought saying, "he can't be trusted Gabby." Keeping the thought inside of my head, even after all that happened after Bonteau's hit; subconsciously my heart still pumped full of love for the man that I'd eventually have to kill. I'd mourn my love's death, but I agreed with Brody on only one idea; Minos Tiernan had to die.

Chapter 5

'Sylas'

I was hoping that handing Maggie over to Gabrielle would give me an entrance to show her how much I really cared for her. Magdeline was going to die anyhow so, what better avenue than to allow The Black Widow to make a mess of her as she was so known to do. I'd tried to reach her smart phone again to arrange a meeting with her, but of course she'd disposed of the phone already. Proud of her, I smiled inside of the knowledge I'd engraved into her mind to find a safe haven and remain unseen and unheard of by anyone including me if it need be. Ravaging her former safe haven after my tracking device located her to be the one place I'd expected her to be; I surprisingly didn't find her there. Instead I found the tiny chip I'd installed lying on the desk inside of her security office encased within a small zip-lock bag. It seems I'd trained her a bit too well as she'd moved two steps ahead of me and that bothered me slightly. Apparently she was bold enough to remove it or she'd found a black market physician that was willing to remove it. For the right price those low level docs will do anything you asked them to do. Another problem I needed to attend to was the character Brody that Zindzhi spoke of in our last meeting. I decided that it was time to take trip to my homeland, Africa, to visit my eldest sister to find out if she'd heard or received more information on this man. Once I was inside of the black sedan that was our transportation to her lavish mansion; she embraced me with a kiss of each cheek. "Mon frère, how are you my love?" I return her greeting, "I am well Aida. However, there is a reason for my visit to our homeland that precedes family visits." "This I assumed already," she said. She went on to say, "Business as usual brother. I am aware of your inquiry and I have pinpointed this man that you seek. But, you're not going to like what you hear." I listen intently to Aida and await her important information. "This man, he is linked to your Gabrielle." A look of confusion crossed my face, "Gabby? How is this meant? I'm acquainted with all of Gabrielle's connections open and underground as well." My sister laughs at this declaration lightly; this act has become a norm with my sister as it hadn't before. "*Vous tromper*, I told you this would happen eventually. Your Gabrielle, she is nothing but trouble for you only because of your love for her. This love will equal either your demise or your succession." My sister said as she shook her head at me. "Are you going to tell me? Or are you going to continue to reprimand and lecture me?" I said to her. She continued saying, "The first thing you should know is that this man is bound to a contract from underground grey market slime. The amount on his head is grand in price and is tied to this man's ability discover important information that even I wouldn't be privy to." Adjusting herself in her seat as if that revelation disturbed her she went on to say, "This Brody as I have named to you. His given birth name is Broderick Black." Aida then paused to allow this information to properly sink into my thought process. "Black?" I said in mere confusion. "Black, as in Gabrielle Black?" "Yes," Aida confirmed to me. "But, Aida Gabby has no siblings. I'd checked myself long ago when I first sought to recruit her. She was an only child, her parents her only surviving relatives." Aida spoke then, "Or so you thought Minos." She raised an eyebrow and said to me, "This Broderick is an illegitimate child of the father's. Kept secret for obvious reasons; it seems that she's been in touch with him the entire duration of her employment with The Society. I thought I had killed him there in our meeting in the subway, but it seems he is preservative. He was her inside connect to the black market, grey market, white and beyond; and he has a very keen skill in receiving sensitive information. This is why the price on his head is so extravagantly high." It was hard to fathom that Gabby had been keeping a secret from him since the beginning of their time together. I imagined this is how she managed to fall off of the radar so quickly and so often as of lately. Gabby's brother was a huge surprise to him, but he never proved to be any danger to his person so far. From what he could tell, Broderick's main concern had and has been to protect Gabrielle. So, he and I were on the same note concerning that endeavor. If this guy was willing to risk his life several times over to protect Gabrielle, then his untimely demise would crush her and I wouldn't be able to deal with her having another emotional breakdown. He had to warn her and keep her and her brother intact. "Zindzhi can you still work your wonders as you did previously and find Gabby's smart phone so that I may message her? I have to alert her so that she doesn't get caught in the crossfire." She dropped her head, "Tisk, Tisk, Tisk baby brother." I gave her a look of desperation; she knew the extent of my love for Gabrielle. She also knew that Gabby's death would crush me so hard that I may not recover. "Oui, I can do this for you. But, I warn you if I am privy that you are in any danger I will step in and clean to whole situation. I'm sure you know what that entails and you will not be able to stop this. I will exercise my status to clear every faction and have you step down momentarily. Je compris?" I knew that my older sister had power beyond compromise so I nodded my agreement to her and tried to enjoy the rest of the day with her.

••

The next day I was on my private jet on the way back to the states. I used that time to use the link that Zindzhi had given me to Gabrielle's smart phone and sent her an urgent message. "PLEASE DO NOT SWITCH PHONES AGAIN. I HAVE AN IMPORTANT WARNING FOR YOU. I AM AWARE OF YOUR BROTHER BRODERICK AND HIS POSITION IN ORGANIZATIONS. MY SISTER IS AIDA AND SHE HAS ALERTED ME OF A PRICE ON YOUR BROTHER'S HEAD. I WILL DO WHAT I CAN TO STOP THIS BUT YOU MUST TRUST ME AGAIN GABBY. PLEASE FOR THE SAKE OF YOUR BROTHER'S LIFE. MEET ME AT MY SAFE HAVEN

IN ARIZONA WITH BRODERICK AND WE CAN FIGURE OUT WHO CONTRACTED THE HIT AND ENSURE IT'S NOT FULFILLED. PLEASE GABBY I NEED YOUR TRUST OR YOUR BROTHER WILL DIE VERY SOON. –SYLAS" She replies to my text message, "YOU LEAVE ME NO CHOICE. ARIZONA IN TWO DAYS BRING NO ONE, BUT I WILL BRING BRODERICK AS THIS IS HIS CAUSE." This gave me hope that I could regain the trust she had for me prior to Gerard's hit.

When I arrived at my safe haven in Arizona, one only Gabrielle and I knew of; she was there waiting for me with a huge muscle mass of a man. He looked as if he could've been a football player. But, I knew never to underestimate a man; never mind the size slender or muscular. I imagine they beat me there to check for any traps that they I may have hidden for them. "Greetings

Gabrielle, it's been a while since I've saw you," I said to her. "May we enter? Or would you like the information I've received relayed here in the drive of my safe haven?" The large man spoke, "It's okay Gabby, lets go inside." As I entered Gabby and her brother followed. There was no worry of any attack; I was on my own property and an attack here would be an unwise decision. Not to brag, but I would prove to be a difficult man to take down. We entered to foyer and immediately started speaking, "Firstly, I've been informed that this man is your brother Broderick. I've never made your acquaintance, but I am thankful for you protecting Gabby when she needed it." I went on to say, "Secondly, I've been informed that my sister Aida, known mostly by Zindzhi attempted to attack you Broderick and for that I apologize. When it concerns me she goes a bit overboard and proves to be quite cold hearted and fierce." Just then

Broderick's eyes narrowed, "I'm no worse for the wear," he said to me. On to the important details, "you must have proved to be a worthy adversary because she's warned me of a price contracted for you by a gray market dealer and entered by several others to exceed the contract to a ridiculous amount." Gabby's lips pursed. "Now I don't know what you did in particular but, Aida has told me that you have a knack for finding information that even she cannot become privy to; and Aida is the highest leader that any faction or organization could be placed in. Nothing happens without her knowing. But, apparently you've got a one up on even her radar." Brody folded his arms and spoke, "this is true, go on." I went on to say, "I'm alerting you because the last serious hit Gabby finished broke her bad emotionally and I'm sure the death of her brother would break her into. She doesn't trust me anymore but, I'm hoping that'll change." I pleaded my case, "I've had to be the part of Highest In Command and hold a firm hand Gabby per my sister Aida's plans. Maggie proved to be a sore thorn in my spine; I'd already planned to allow Aida to price her life, but once my sister alerted me that Maggie had initiated a hit on you; I thought it'd be better to allow you the satisfaction." Placing a look of apology on my face I said, "Knowing you as I do, I was sure you'd handle the job properly. I'm no good at apologies, but this is as close as I can get to asking you to instill your trust in me once more." One nod from Gabby was all I got and that was enough for me. Moving toward my wet bar I poured myself a glass of Brandy and dropped two ice cubes inside. "Now that we've cleared that up; we've got to figure out what to do about this contract on Broderick. It can be handled but there will be a wide range of mess and one hell of a clean up involved." Gabby walked beside me and said, "I think I could use one of those too. You should put one back too Brody, after this info you deserve a stiff one." I turned to grab two tumblers and the bottle of Brandy and felt a tiny sting in the side of my neck. Before I had the chance to turn and defend myself, my world went black, my body went limp, and I fell hard to the ground. This was not how I thought my death would be. But, the devil had always had a seat on the throne right next to his all along.

Gabrielle

'The Future'

As Sylas turned to his wet bar, he was relaxed and calm and sure of himself. He was content with regaining my trust. His guard one fraction too loose and that was his biggest mistake. He never heard Brody approach him from behind as he grabbed the Brandy to pour us a drink. In one swift move, Broderick entered a needle into Sylas' neck that contained enough tranquilizers to put down a large lion. We had another needle on spare just in case he awoke to soon. We tied his arms and legs and gagged his mouth thoroughly. Broderick threw Sylas' body over his shoulder and entered the closed garage door and threw the limp mass into the back of our Land Rover complete with a thick wired cage just as police cruisers carried and dark tint to conceal the inside passengers. Just as he'd placed Sylas into the truck a phone chirped. It was Sylas's smart phone; Broderick grabbed it and threw it inside of the house onto the kitchen counter. There one was deadly mistake that my brother and I overlooked however. We overlooked the insertion of the tracking device that was inside of Sylas someplace. The same device he'd had placed inside of me should I manage to be missing. Once we were highway bound, little did we know; Minos' sister Aida had assumed something was afoot once her brother hadn't answered her original message.

She sent a code afterwards that was an emergency word to alert one another of danger. When he answered neither message, she started the device that would track her brother's chip. Immediately she was on a jet bound to America and intent on killing that bitch Gabrielle. She knew immediately that his little bitch had done her brother foul and just as she told him; if she was forced to become involved it would be of major proportions. She planned to clean every faction and organization until she found her brother and the erase of everything that had been in her path.

■■■

I was the future. The Society would answer to me now that Magdeline and Minos were no longer present. As Second in command, I would become The Highest In Command. No one was left to stop me. Brody and I had plans and they were of major proportions.

<u>Book 3</u>

<u>Broderick's Story</u>

<u>'Relative, Love, and Blood'</u>

<u>Coming Soon!</u>

Made in the USA
Middletown, DE
06 May 2021